GUY GOF

Forever Nude

TRANSLATED FROM THE FRENCH
by Frank Wynne

VINTAGE BOOKS
London

Published by Vintage 2009

2 4 6 8 10 9 7 5 3 1

Copyright © Éditions Gallimard, 1998
English translation copyright © Frank Wynne, 2008

Guy Goffette has asserted his right under the Copyright, Designs and
Patents Act 1988 to be identified as the author of this work

First published in French under the title *Elle, par Bonheur, et
toujours nue* by Éditions Gallimard, Paris, France

First published by William Heinemann in 2008

Vintage
Random House, 20 Vauxhall Bridge Road,
London SW1V 2SA

www.vintage-books.co.uk

Addresses for companies within The Random House Group Limited
can be found at: www.randomhouse.co.uk/offices.htm

The Random House Group Limited Reg. No. 954009

A CIP catalogue record for this book
is available from the British Library

ISBN 9780099471981

The Random House Group Limited supports The Forest
Stewardship Council (FSC), the leading international forest
certification organisation. All our titles that are printed on
Greenpeace approved FSC certified paper carry the FSC logo.
Our paper procurement policy can be found at
www.rbooks.co.uk/environment

Printed in the UK by CPI Bookmarque, Croydon, CR0 4TD

The translator would like to express his gratitude to the Centre National du Livre, for its generous support during the translation of this book.

This book is supported by the French Ministry of Foreign Affairs as part of the Burgess programme run by the Cultural Department of the French Embassy in London. www.frenchbooknews.com

Liberté • Égalité • Fraternité
RÉPUBLIQUE FRANÇAISE

Ouvrage publié avec le concours du Ministère Français chargé de la culture – Centre National du Livre

This work is published with the assistance of the French Ministry responsible for Culture – The National Book Centre

For Philo and Franz Bartelt

For Bernadette and Philippe Coquelet

In painting too, truth is close to error.

Pierre Bonnard

Forgive me, Pierre, but Marthe was mine from the first. Like a young whelp plunging into field of ripe corn when storm threatens, scampering and wallowing, I threw myself into her.

You must understand, I was alone, caught at a loose end between trains in a northern town trampled by the summer sun. I wandered into a museum a stone's throw from the train station, whose colonnades and imperious façade towered over the town square. I was looking for adventure and cool shade and thought that in this temple of sorts I would surely find a sanctuary of shadows and silence for one sick at heart.

As I stepped into one of the galleries, still hounded by the heat, constantly dabbing at my neck, my face, my hands — I saw her. Or rather I saw a young woman come towards me, about whom I knew nothing other than that she was nude, that she was beautiful, and her radiance suddenly cooled me and revived me. She turned her body slowly towards the light of a great picture window, towards the falling snow of the muslin drapes and, as she turned, arched against the sunlight, the scent of her body showered me like an armful of wet ferns and my knees gave out from under me. I had to sit down, my head swimming as if from heatstroke. Suddenly the scent of eau de Cologne filled the room and trickled down my neck.

At that moment, Pierre, before I could make the slightest movement, before I could reach out my hand, lift the gauzy veil of dust which separated me from her, Marthe was mine.

I forgot the rose-pink divan, the mirror and the bathtub which you carefully arranged about her like homage paid to a queen, forgot that this was simply a painting, that this Eve in black ballet pumps, standing with her weight on one leg, buttocks quivering, nipples erect, was no more than a piece of painted canvas measuring 124 cm by 108 cm, a picture in a gallery. I forgot everything, the time, the walls, the sweltering heat of the city, my faltering life, what I had come here to find. Everything.

I forgot everything, because a woman's voice, suddenly breaking the silence, had with one bright stroke wiped from my memory every other woman I had known; because, with a single gesture, she revealed to me the meaning of the word woman, a meaning which predates memory, inflames desire and gives it form and colour — a meaning which many will go to their graves without ever having glimpsed.

Truth be told, though I did not know it then, I had been waiting for this moment, this oblivion, for forty-seven years. I had long since put away childish things, left behind my paintbox, moved beyond the eyes of the child I had been and traded the shimmer and dazzle of paint for the bitter ink of words.

Yet here she stood within my grasp, bright and blazing and more naked still than falling water, and here I stood, suddenly alive. I no longer felt the weight of my body fettering my wings. I took a step towards Marthe, and for an instant something flickered in the little painted mirror above the washbasin. Was it you, Pierre, or was it the reflection on my wings?

Then just as suddenly, everything was as before. The mirror now reflected only the chair and beside it, Marthe, pale as death, the reflection of her mortal body without the face of Venus. I suddenly felt as if there were someone beside me, I turned. No one. But at that moment I heard the sound of hurried footsteps on a stair, a clap of thunder, then another, and the light was swallowed up in a great silence. A storm had blown the fuses. I hurried for the exit.

Outside, the street was dark. It was raining hard. As I crossed the road, I glimpsed a woman in a red dress trying to make her way between the cars. A tram sounded its klaxon. I called to her with every fibre of my being.

3

I called out her name, Pierre, a name I had never known, or one I had forgotten long ago. Marthe, perhaps, or Marie. Forgive me, Pierre, forgive me: Marie or Marthe; Marthe or Marie, call her what you will, she was your gift to me, Pierre, she was the field of ripe corn where I could shelter from the storm. And from the first moment I saw her, I possessed her. She, by happy chance, forever nude.

A Christmas Tale

I

Paris, December 1893.

The young woman who stands there, hesitating, on the kerb is but is not her.

One step forward, two steps back, she vacillates as she attempts to cross the Boulevard Haussmann. From the thunder and the clamour of hoofs it sounds like a racetrack and looks as though every horse-drawn vehicle in Paris, every brougham, tram, and omnibus has converged on this one boulevard where they scrabble for some scrap of cobbled street.

One step forward, two steps back, already she is Marthe and yet she is still Marie.

Twice today she has almost been knocked down and trampled by the horses. But she is stubborn and will not be cowed. Besides, in spite of her winter coat and her mittens she is cold, the leather of her ankle boots is thin and her feet are cramped and frozen.

She has just finished at the florist and her fingers are still aching from standing in a dark, poorly heated room all day threading artificial leaves and petals onto wire stems.

How wrong you were, Marie, to think that you would find happiness and fortune here in Paris. You should have stayed home in le Berry tending pigs with your father. There, at least the flowers are real, they spring up from the lush, vast, verdant earth; there, the summer is golden as a wedding ring on a young girl's finger, there, the winter is starch-white, a fire burns in the grate and horse-drawn carriages are so rare that you know each one by sight and doff your bonnet as they pass.

Enough of these foolish thoughts, Marie. Stop hesitating. Step out onto the Boulevard Haussmann. It's now or never.

2

For someone who has made walking an art, someone who adjusts his stride to the unfolding drama of the streets as a poet refines his metre, any moment, any time of day may prove auspicious. Today, that moment is now. Never mind that the temperature has dipped cruelly below zero, the sky is so high that the city now looks like a frightened mouse scuttling along the skirting board, beneath the lampshades of the streetlights.

He smiles at this image and thinks again of the Seine, where he has just been walking, the leaden slowness of the water dull as the discarded blade of a barber's cut-throat razor. He decides to sketch the image on his pad.

Indifferent to the cold, he takes out his pad, his stub of pencil and, leaning against a wall like a village policeman, adds this image to the sketches with which he will delight his dear friend Vuillard at the studio tomorrow. Already he can see Vuillard's smile lift the corners of his red beard, hear him exclaim without a hint of irony: An excellent crop, Pierre!

Especially this sketch here. I see you didn't waste your day, you rogue!

This has been his daily routine ever since he became a free man, ever since he became an artist. Come rain, wind or hail, Pierre prowls the streets of Paris, from morning to night, from Batignolles to Montparnasse, from Pantin to Montmartre just to set his eyes straight, to bathe his soul in the winding current of the Seine, in the tumult of the streets.

Paris is his canvas and his brushes are the shadows and light, charcoal or graphite on tremulous paper; ladies' legs which make the earth shake beneath their frills and finery.

Nothing escapes him. Here, a fleeting, furtive gesture, there a vast comic scene. A little laundress dressed in black, bent double beneath the weight of her laundry; a conference of dogs fighting over an invisible bone; a carriage horse at rest, craning its neck to graze on the flowery hat of a lady scandalised by the behaviour of a little girl in pink on the other side of the road. A shop front and its yellow awning, the lettering reversed; a passing lady and her lapdog struggling against the querulous wind which looks as though it might undress her, their tussle a dance of curved lines and drunken colour against the horizon.

Now, just three paces away, he sees a young girl in a winter coat steadying her nerves to plunge into the middle of the Boulevard Haussmann, into the crowd, into the night.

3

Now or never. Sometimes there is no 'now or never', sometimes they become one and something that was not destined to happen happens just the same. Afterwards, all you can say is that you never saw it coming.

Now. The youthful Marthe dives into the crowd as though into a lake, leaving behind Marie whose heart-rending homesickness she carries like a shadow in her heart, Marie who comes back, claws at her on nights when she is weary.

She did not realise that the thundering traffic had started up again and now she finds herself stuck midway across Boulevard Haussmann, caught up in the teeming flow of carriages, not knowing who she is or why she is here, turning every which way like a weather-vane buffeted by the four winds, desperately seeking the true north that is the far side of the boulevard, longing for the calm, the warmth of her room. Paris deceived her with its promise of bright lights, of frills and flounces. Now she finds herself alone, her heart heaving in her throat, as carriages hurtle and a hundred frantic horses gallop past.

As her heart beats wildly in her chest, Marthe hears Marie spluttering and coughing, scolding her in a shrill voice:

You see, you can show off, you can play at being a lady all you like but listen to your heart, your heart doesn't lie. The doctor was right, but you just went right ahead and did what you pleased. Remember what the doctor said? 'You need rest and fresh air, mademoiselle Marie, you need to stay in the country or you'll not go far.'

'But doctor I'm twenty years old, I want to live. I want to live!'

Now, there is a steam tram rushing straight towards you, klaxon blaring, can you hear it, Marthe? Can you hear it?

4

When he hears the frantic blasts of the tram's horn, Pierre realises the danger this foolish girl had put herself in and dashes into the boulevard to rescue her.

Now, safe on the far side of the street, Pierre looks at her and realises she is the one. Beneath a bonnet now slightly askew which she fumbles to adjust – awkward fingers, delicate hatpins – she has the fierce look of a cornered animal, a tuft of auburn hair peeks out from her bonnet, her pink face is furrowed, her feline eyes blink with gratitude. God, how beautiful she is! Slight and graceful in spite of the thick coat, she looks to Pierre to be no more than sixteen.

She has not said a word, she is struggling still to catch her breath, she simply looks up at this dashing young man as if he were her safe haven, this man who towers over her, smiling, with eyes as wide and black as a child's. Behind his steel-rimmed pince-nez, his eyes look like glass beads set upon velvet. Pierre is dressed like a gentleman. Were it not for the greatcoat thrown over his shoulders, which makes him look older, and the bowler hat which doesn't suit his face, she would guess he was no more than twenty. There is something of a boy about him, judging by the sparse beard, still mostly down, and the adolescent way his eyes seem to devour her.

You are wrong, Marie. The one whom fate has chosen to be here, in the right place, at the right time, is a man: although he is young, he is single-minded, he lives for the moment. At twenty (he is twenty-six now), in spite of the opposition of his friends, his family, the woman he loved, he chose freedom, he chose to paint, he chose to turn his back on the future, that little grey train that rumbles monotonously, predictably into the sunset.

5

A few days after earning a first-class degree in Greek, Latin and Philosophy, Pierre informed his father that he wanted to enrol in the École des Beaux-Arts. Eugène, his father, was furious, he was thunderstruck, he all but had a fit of apoplexy! Seeing her husband scowl Pierre's mother felt suddenly faint and glanced around her for somewhere to set down the long-stemmed glass in her trembling hand. When the Chief Clerk at the Ministry of War frowned, his busy eyebrows met above his forbidding pince-nez, as though he had just been told that the enemy was at the city gates.

Pierre can remember watching the cap his father wore pulled down over his forehead – like Sainte-Beuve – rising inexorably under the force of incredulity. 'What? You would choose the life of an artist when you have been all but called to the bar? Surely you cannot be serious, Pierre? Come, come, you shall study law, and we shall say no more about this.'

It is futile to defy his father, unseemly even to protest;

Pierre knows what he must do. He feigns acquiescence, lowers his eyes, but behind his back he keeps two fingers crossed: he who laughs last laughs longest.

And since he also has two hands, he uses the left to hastily apply to study Law even as his right hand is applying to study at the Académie Julian. Papa knows nothing of this: in September 1887, he has other things to worry about, what with the constant vying for power in government and his own minister, Général Boulanger, up to his old tricks.

Let Pierre live with his grandmother at 8 rue de Parme if it pleases him, let him walk arm in arm with Paris like a schoolgirl, Eugène Bonnard does not care so long as his son passes his law exams, takes up public office and gives his father the respect that is his due.

Three years later, it is done. Pierre qualifies as a lawyer and, though his heart is not in it, he works part time at the Paris Registry Office. In 1890 he transfers to the Parquet de la Seine to work at the ministry, though this too does not hold him long. For though he does not yet know what he wants, he knows it is not this.

Not this living death shut up behind these tall windows, surrounded by musty files and men who at thirty are already old, hunched over their desks spending their days poring over legal niceties, useful as a bald man's comb. Not this life lived constantly at heel, marching to the beat of another man's

drum, endlessly kowtowing and tugging the forelock, with
no reward in sight but the prospect of a medal of long service
to be hung next to the law degree in the garishly wallpa-
pered living room. Not this life of leather elbow-patches,
drab paintings, castors on the furniture and carpet slippers.

He wants to live. To experience everything that life can
mean. To be singular, free, untamed.

What attracted me, he will say later, *was not really art, but
the wild extravagance of the artist's life as I imagined it, to be free
to do as one pleases. It's true I had long been drawn to painting
and drawing, but it was not my overwhelming passion; more than
anything, I wanted to escape the monotony of life.*

'More than anything' is easily said. But what of the hunger,
the cold, the loneliness, the disillusionment of the morning
after? All these things his father has drummed into him, but
in vain. The most beautiful eyes in all the world are those of
freedom, and nothing – not money nor glory – will dissuade
Pierre from pursuing his dream. If they were to offer him
the Légion d'honneur, he would politely decline. He desperately wants anything but a pot-bound life of insignificant loves
and armchair travelling. And he wants for nothing, after all,
he has two eyes, two legs, and all of Paris.

Paris for him alone. Paris spread before him, to dazzle
his eyes, to teach his fingers. Paris is his easel.

6

It is not because he is a new to Paris that Pierre stands wonderstruck, even in the grey skies and the cold. After all, he has been living here for eighteen years now, and though he saw nothing of the city in his years in boarding school at the Lycée Louis-le-Grand and the Lycée Charlemagne or almost nothing – a scrap of sky over the playground, occasional, awkward supervised day-trips – he has spent every day in the decade since he left school tramping the streets of this city, and each one of those days has brought its share of treasure for his sketchpad, its share of gold.

Now, suddenly, a rich seam of gold has opened up before him, he can scarcely believe his eyes. Suddenly nothing exists, nothing but the miracle that is this girl who stands before him, this vision which casts him out of earth, of heaven.

Are they standing on the kerb amid the milling crowds,

or sitting at a café table amid the smoke and clamour? He would be hard pressed to say, if indeed he were capable of speech. Already he sees Paris as a shifting body of desire, tossing and turning between the sheets.

7

Already, Pierre knows but does not know that the young woman who basks in the warmth of his eyes will take him to the limits of himself. Already he knows but does not know that the rising tide of a woman's eyes can turn the world upside down, that no dam can hold it back, especially when that dam is a living, breathing man quivering like a cello string in the azure light. Already he knows but does not know that the tide is primordial, is woman, is naked, that in her all colours are washed in darkness to bloom again in the light.

Now, he simply gazes at this girl as he has never gazed on anyone before, unless perhaps in some other life he can no longer remember. The world itself begins again with her and he is reborn. A sapling in the sunlight waiting for its leaves to burst forth before it speaks. Waiting to flower.

She is so beautiful, so tender, with such an impish silence that, laughing, he might have named her Marie.

FOREVER NUDE

But it is she who breaks the silence, a rush of words pouring into the blue air, she who, with a single breath, without a blush, says: 'My name is Marthe de Méligny. You can call me Marthe.'

8

Marthe de Méligny is the name of an aristocrat, the name of a courtesan, it is not her name.

Even if her eyes were filled with all the gold in heaven and on earth, her every gesture swathed in Calais lace, and her voice clear and pure as spring water, she would fool no one. And indeed she makes no attempt to be convincing.

But when Pierre looks at her – looks at her as if she were the one perfect flower in the bouquet – she can forget where she has come from, her past disgrace, her present penury.

She talks. She laughs, and Pierre hangs on her every word. He is staring so deeply into her green eyes that the words sound like pebbles tumbling through reflections, amid the grass. Whether she is who she says she is – the daughter of an Italian nobleman whose only request when he died was that she should go to Paris to earn her living – does not matter to him as long as her red lips move, as long as time stands still, as long as they sit here facing each other, the sea face to face with the sea.

When at last he gets to his feet, night has fallen. He takes her hand and walking upon the water, he says: 'My name is Pierre, Pierre Bonnard. I am an artist.'

Minor Prophets

. . . and the blue incense of wan horizons?
Stéphane Mallarmé

9

A dwarf stands in the street, staring at the wall. He has been standing there for some time, his eyes rolled heavenward, arms flailing wildly. Passers-by turn to look at the little man: his bushy beard beneath a black, broad-brimmed hat, his walking stick raised, he mutters half-formed sentences, turning his head this way and that: 'PB, PB, PB who? Who in *non de non* is this PB?'

Gradually a crowd begins to form, they gather some distance away and watch him, wondering, laughing at him, all of which simply serves to further agitate this little scrap of a man, whose flamboyant outfit – thick orange corduroy trousers, red shirt and scarf – makes him look like a clown.

In fact, the cause of all this commotion is a poster, an advertisement for champagne. On a vast yellow and white background, beneath a troupe of dancing black letters which she marshals with her fan, a laughing woman with a daringly low-cut dress and a shock of brilliant red hair holds aloft a champagne glass which brims over in cataracts of bubbles.

'Magnificent!' exclaims the dwarf, jumping for joy as the crowd stare incredulously, their eyes flitting between the gnome and the poster.

'Do you know who painted this? Does anyone here know who this man is who hides behind these intertwined initials?' The crowd begin to back away from this loon, begin to disappear, to disappear into the background, leaving behind them the excitable little man, his cane twirling like the vanes of the windmill at the Moulin-Rouge.

Paris may be vast, but the world of art is small. It did not
take long for Toulouse-Lautrec – the dwarf whom the gawping
crowd did not recognise – to discover the identity of PB.
Who but Pierre Bonnard? How had he not thought of it
earlier? He already knew the man by name, had seen a number
of his paintings at the *Salon des Indépendants*, but advertising
posters? Never. And a poster of such daring, such assurance!

Henri de Toulouse-Lautrec, known by everyone in Paris
as *le nabot*, the dwarf, first encounters the young Bonnard at
28 rue Pigalle, where Pierre shares a small studio with Maurice
Denis and Édouard Vuillard. Lugné-Poe[1] drops by from time
to time to rehearse his plays. Pierre had met Denis and
Vuillard four years earlier, in 1887, at the Académie Julian,
where they and their friends – Sérusier, Ranson, Ibels – re-
invented the paintbrush as a musical instrument, and as they
played, art was transformed. They condemned the Académie,
denounced every school of painting – including Impressionism,
a movement which they knew only by name. They are twenty

years old, they are the new blood, and they want all the world
to know it. All the old men with their paint-pots and their
self-important daubs who make gallery walls drool and critics
swoon: the Flandrins and the Cormons and the Bastien-
Lepages, the Carolus-Durans whom the critics rank as talents
greater than Delacroix and Ingres. And Bonnat whom
Monsieur Thiers, destroyer of the Paris Commune, dandled
on his knee. Meissonier and even Bouguereau whom Gauguin
in fearsome manner, declared 'amounts to zero'.

Indeed Paul Sérusier, the most fervent thinker of the
group, who cannot speak for theorising, believes that the
success of their revolution is in Gauguin's hands. From Pont-
Aven, Sérusier brought back *Le Talisman* – a small landscape
painted in flat pure colours on a cigar-box cover under the
watchful eye of the master. And Gauguin said let there be
light, and there was light. Gauguin's message is clear: from
henceforth let your green be green and your blue be blue,
'the most beautiful green in your palette', the most beautiful blue.

Maurice Denis, the other duty theoretician, then decrees
that 'a painting – before it is a war horse, a nude, a scene –
is essentially a flat surface covered with colours assembled in
a certain order.'

Eureka, painting has been discovered, painting is born!
All that remains now is to bring the good news to the waiting

world. It is our role to play Isaiah. Sérusier, stumbling into prophecy, rose solemnly to his feet: 'We are the minor prophets, we are *Les Nabis*.'

Nabi is catchy, pretty, a little mysterious and much better than 'prophet' or at least is less pretentious, less ridiculous. Let's go for Les Nabis. Everyone cheers and Pierre feels happier than he has since his schooldays: at seventeen no one is terribly serious.

For now, let us simply enjoy the festivities, let us spend some time in Nabyssinia as we await the arrival of Vuillard and his red beard, of Ker-Xavier Roussel, the 'Breton Casanova', of Verkade from the Netherlands and Ballin from Denmark, of Vallotton from Switzerland and Rippl-Rónai from Hungary. Once they have arrived, it will seem as though Les Nabis have taken over the planet.

While we wait for Maillol.

While we wait for the revolution to grow fat and for things, as they invariably do, to fall apart.

I I

Le nabot has no time for les Nabis. Nor, at heart, does Bonnard, who often allows his mind to wander during their meetings. While Sérusier speaks with passion, Pierre stands by himself, usually by the window, rolls a cigarette and puffs away, dreaming of God knows what.

Perhaps of the Japanese print he glimpsed in the window of Siegfried Bing on the rue Chauchat, which intrigues him. The consummate grace of the line distils colours to their purest form and they float away like butterflies. This is what he too strives for: colour that might express movement, light and feeling. To the devil with Gauguin, his heavy lines and his flat garish colours.

I realised, he would later tell Gaston Diehl, *that everything could be expressed by colour with no need to resort to depth or texture. It seemed to me that it was possible to translate light, forms, and character using nothing but colour, without recourse to values.*

Ever since Pierre began working with lithography, engravings, fabrics, he has Japanese kimonos fluttering in his head.

True, the fashion in *fin-de-siècle* Paris is for Japanese this and Japanese that – mostly for 'Japanese tat'. Since he is poor, Bonnard capitalises on the fashion to earn *quelques sous*: decorating fans, screens, furniture, ceramics and stained glass in the Japanese style. Two birds with one stone – the work affords him a measure of financial independence and allows him to perfect his palette – Gauguin does not have a monopoly on colour. It is this which earns Bonnard the nickname *the Nipponese Nabi*.

He has already painted a number of canvases in which Japanese style has matured into a style all his own – more or less. Less, in *Boules de Neige* in which the Japanese artist Utamaro can still be seen peeking through; more, in *Les Femmes au chien*, a vivid and sensual frontal composition, in which everything he loves and will ever love – women, nature, animals, chequerboard motifs – pours forth in a wild ecstasy.

But Bonnard only truly becomes *Bonnard* in his lithographs, his posters in particular. In these, Pierre allows PB a mastery of line, a lightness of touch and a fluidity of colour. In three years, he will paint no fewer than two hundred and fifty posters. Of these, one will make his name and earn him, together with money, his family's respect and his father's blessing: this is the poster for *France-Champagne*, and it is this which, in 1891, will have the dwarf they call 'Monsieur Toulouse' jumping for joy in the middle of a Paris street.

At the Lumière brothers' cinematograph four years later, the image of the tall thin man and the plump dwarf walking side by side would have everyone rolling in the aisles, but this afternoon, as they walk through the streets of Paris, barely anyone notices them.

Toulouse-Lautrec is done up to the nines, wearing the formal attire he always wears when he frequents the brothels of Paris. In the brothels Toulouse-Lautrec's diminutive size makes him lord of all he surveys, he does not have to stoop, his mouth is at the perfect height to kiss the breasts of any whore who comes near. Pierre now stoops a little to hear him smile and say again how delighted he is to have discovered Pierre, how happy he is that they have met.

They are heading to the offices of Ancourt at 83 rue Faubourg-Saint-Denis. It was Ancourt who printed Pierre's poster for *France-Champagne* and 'Monsieur Toulouse' is impatient to meet him, for he is convinced that he has at last found his path, convinced that by tomorrow he and his *Moulin*

Rouge poster of the dancer '*La Goulue*' will be the talk of Paris.

On the way back, dancing and twirling his cane, Toulouse-Lautrec invites his friend to come and meet '*les filles*'. Happily, Pierre, who is incapable of telling a lie, has a perfect excuse: he has to attend his weekly service at 'the Temple'.

'The Temple' is the Nabis name for the studio of Paul Ranson the Nabi occultist, where they meet every Saturday. These assemblies are presided over by Madame Ranson, the sacred 'light of the Temple'. They come, as they do to the monthly dinners, dressed in Oriental costumes.

Pierre's natural reticence and modesty means that he often remains aloof from the debates, though if some absent friend is criticised, he is quick to intervene. Pierre has a flair for making others feel at ease. His roguishness, his keen wit and his imagination are all the more surprising since they seem at odds with his appearance. From his gangling frame, goatee beard, and pince-nez one would think him reserved, inscrutable. The Nabis hang on his every word, especially Ker Roussel, the philandering Nabi, and Édouard Vuillard, the faithful companion.

Édouard and Pierre, working side by side in their studio on the rue Pigalle, inspire each other. The warm, enthusiastic critiques of the former are invariably met either with smiling silence or eloquent grimaces by the latter. Yet the two men have a perfect affinity, their respect for one another is immense. They hold each other in such high regard that they will never address each other as *'tu'*, preferring the more formal *'vous'*.

In the beginning they tend to be lumped together. It is a mistake, for though they inevitably share similar influences and a similar worldview, their subject matter and their styles quickly will diverge. Vuillard, the extrovert, will retreat into a style of nostalgic intimism, his lavish palette luxuriating in every subtle nuance of the muted gamut of his colours. Bonnard, the introvert, by contrast will throw open every window onto the radiant field of colours illuminating Marthe, and the world.

Marthe's induction into the Temple will all but sound the death knell for this charming carnival.

Draped in royal purple, or in canary yellow, here was a woman whose mere presence would slowly extinguish the 'light of the Temple' even as the fire in Pierre's eyes begins to blaze.

She happily accompanies her lover among the prophets, but quickly feels like Susanna at her bath[2], in spite of what Denis, who takes a Bible to bed with him, may think.

Having all these eyes on her reawakens her old fears. She is afraid that these men will see right through her, will see the little country girl hiding behind the tattered screen of the name de Méligny. She is afraid that they will wake Marie, who sleeps the sleep of the just in her childhood home, on her father's farm.

It is at this point that Marthe begins to avoid people, to retreat from society, dragging Pierre in her wake, gradually cutting him off from his friends, driving them away with her moods. The only ones who meet with her approval are Vuillard, whose conversation she finds enchanting, and Ker Roussel, the handsome libertine who makes her laugh, but in time she will drive them away too. She will lock herself in her kitchen when they visit, or in her bedroom or her bathroom, constantly complaining just like the biblical Martha, until in time she becomes an ill-tempered shrew constantly harping on vague and vain recriminations.

Her delicate health plays no small part in her behaviour: she is highly strung and has a lump in her breast which saps her breath and causes her to cough. Her doctor is not optimistic, he thinks she will not live long, but the future is as fleeting as sparks showering from a firework. Martha will outlive her doctor.

But what can you do when you have been told you don't have long to live, when the only man who ever captured your heart is surrounded by people who take up all his time, when all you have is hope for some magical cure? What can you do but tear him away from his friends with every weapon in your arsenal, with kisses and promises and tears? What can you do when you are no more than a burning itch in his skin, constantly railing against that most fearsome mistress, art? What can you do but become his bed, his linen sheets, his sweat, the feral beauty of his eye and his consuming passion?

The Only Garden

'Shhh! If we make a sound time will start up again.'
Paul Claudel

15

Through the winter of '93, Pierre's room blossoms beneath the Paris sky. There are fresh roses in every vase, rich fabrics draped on every chair, silk stockings drying over the wood stove and, behind the screen, a single flower lies between rumpled sheets, a flower that is longer, more naked, lying in the arms of Morpheus: Marthe.

Let her linger in the shades awhile, lulled by dreams in which she floats as in an ocean. In the kitchen, Pierre is making coffee. He likes this moment when the day decides to leap the hurdle of night, when the world is so close to silence that, leaning out of the window, one might hear it breathe. He loves the waiting, the act of pouring the boiling water, as rain and time run in rivulets along the rooftops where only the brick-red necks of the chimneys stand proud like crowing cocks. Slowly the coffee trickles through, black as a punch to the face: night is dead.

Whether or not he is in love, Pierre gets up early afraid that he might miss that meeting with the light, when his eye, still thick with dreams, is like a new-laid egg hidden beneath the straw of his eyelashes.

See him lean over the table at dawn, hastily sketching what impassioned night has fired in his blood, he is a monk in his cell. A joyful monk performing matins after his own fashion, listening to the gurgling of the coffee and the rustle of sheets as sister Marthe turns over in bed.

16

Like all true flowers, Marthe needs little to thrive: a peaceful plot of earth, a little light and lots of water. For the light, there are Pierre's eyes; for the water, there is a small *cabinet de toilette* with a tub until they get a proper bathroom, where Marthe bathes several times a day as though she were never clean, never entirely free of this taint which clings to her skin. As for the plot of earth, Pierre has promised her a surprise this summer.

For the rest, she can do without bourgeois comforts, riches, company. Pierre is cut from the same cloth: he has no need of an Empire sofa or heavy drapes with gold tiebacks nor even an easel. Why not a black cape, a broad-brimmed fedora and a gaucho scarf? No, all Pierre needs is a window, a chair on which to sit, a table at which to eat, a bed on which to sleep. Nothing which will clutter up his life. Four walls are enough and a handful of books which he reads and rereads; his favourite books – Villon and La Fontaine – lie on the nightstand by his bed.

The apartment on the rue Lepic is too small to have company, they go out to see friends: to plays at Lugné-Poe's new theatre L'Oeuvre, to visit the Nabis at home, to see Ambroise Vollard at his boutique or the newcomers, the Natansons, at the offices of *La Revue Blanche*.

The magazine is edited by Thadée Natanson with his brother, who publish in it younger talents – Gide, Proust and Apollinaire – and *La Revue Blanche* also publishes two poets whose work will mark Bonnard for life: Verlaine and Mallarmé.

Thandée discovered Bonnard at the Salon des Indépendants: four small panels[3] were enough to shake him to the core. He fell head over heels, as he will later put it. Pierre is happy to do anything for Thandée: magazine covers, tailpieces, frontispieces, he even provides illustrations for a book – *Marie* by the Danish writer Peter Nansen – for whom Marthe served as a model.

Thandée's wife, Misia, is beautiful, sophisticated and very attractive. Bonnard will paint a number of highly coloured and yet somewhat stilted portraits of her, as though something in her solemn beauty, in her graciousness, perturbs Pierre's natural exuberance.

Truth be told, Marthe is his whole palette.

17

The air you yearned for, Marthe, the earth and the wild flowers,
the trees and the birds, here they are, they are my gift to you.

And she is genuinely surprised. As they drive into Grand-
Lemps, between the blue veil drawn by the hills and the green
ocean where the flatlands stretch away, Marthe can no longer
tell who is looking out through her eyes.

There is a little girl in clogs dancing inside her head,
her heart is beating wildly, she thought that little girl died
when she became Marthe, when Pierre first fell in love
with her, she wants to stop the girl from skipping, from
singing to herself *Oh, la menteuse, elle est amoureuse.* She
wants to look at Pierre, smiling at the wheel, to tell him
again how much she loves him, confess that she has lied to
him. But she is afraid of losing this man who has saved her.
Feverishly, she touches his hand to reassure him. He does
not understand the gesture and looks at her, suddenly
worried.

Happily, they are coming into Le Clos, the imposing family

mansion in the Dauphiné to which Pierre returns every summer to get some colour and visit his family.

The family are all present and correct, just as in *L'après-midi bourgeoise* which Pierre will paint in 1900. Grandmother Mertzdorff is wearing a new outfit for the occasion: a blue dress with a white leafy pattern, a feathered hat. She is watchful, vigilant, radiant in the midst of her brood. There are children everywhere, there is sobbing, shouting and screaming from the edge of the pond, laughter and music pour from every window, hens cackle in the great flowerbeds, cats purr and dogs stand obediently to heel. Eugène, wearing a straw hat, sits in a rattan chair smoking his pipe. Perhaps Charles, the elder brother, is there too, and Andrée, the youngest, with her husband Claude Terrasse, the professor of music whose company so delights Pierre that he will come to love musical notation – though he will never do more than illustrate the music primer Claude has just devised for teaching children.

There are the servants, constantly scurrying past, and the gardener mopping his brow; the treetops are singing, the flowers laughing, roses, fuchsias, ivy clinging to the walls and windfallen fruit you could sink your teeth into. There is that which we believe will last forever but dies the moment our back is turned: the paradise of childhood.

18

The dogs prick up their ears, get to their feet and start to bark; the cats scatter. By the time Pierre's car draws to a halt and the car door slams, the stage, as if by some enchantment, is deserted. The prodigal son has returned, everything is for him. Marthe retreats into the background, where she will remain.

Pierre tells his family that this woman is the love of his life, and when he tells them, there is a joy in his eyes that would melt marble. But it is useless, Marthe is not of their world and she knows it. The family welcome is polite but cool. Pierre feels hurt and angry, determined that they will cut short their stay and go in search of a garden of their own, a garden where they can play at Adam and Eve, can photograph each other mother-naked.

Never mind that his mother has set up a studio in an upstairs room, never mind the laughter and the chatter of the dinner table, the evenings spent by the lamplight, the childhood that lingers still with the goldfish and the reflections in the pond beneath the trees. A time comes when we must leave, when we no longer remember the dappled rainbow of our childhood tears.

They will seek out gardens elsewhere, trees and flowers and water, In Montval, in Médan and Villennes, later at l'Étang-la-Ville, then at Vernouillet near Paris. Too far from Paris, perhaps, to truly feel at home, too close to feel truly in the countryside. Eventually, in 1912, they will fly the nest and buy a little villa perched on a Normandy hillside at Vernonnet, near Veron, with a garden at the back of the house and in front, down the hill, a branch of the Seine where they can go boating. They call it Ma Roulotte.

Here they will come, when they are not travelling, to spend their summers; they will keep their apartment in Paris and the studio on the rue de Douai because, for Pierre, Norman paradise does not begin until July.

19

The kingdom of childhood lives on within each of us, filled with voices and colours, majestic still although the king has long been dethroned and exiled. It brings life to the deserts of old age, its music gives succour to the blind, its images bring comfort to the deaf.

Memory is a secret garden. Everything that is missing from our lives, the great void opening up behind us that fills us with regret, remorse, with yearning, can be likened to a garden. There are trees and grasses there, and flowerbeds, perhaps there is some dark corner into which we do not venture, a place which frightens us precisely because we are drawn to it. It was probably in that dark place that the secret of our future destiny was sealed, to know it would mean to die on the spot.

From Le Clos in Grand-Lemps to the pink house in Cannet, Pierre will always strive to recapture what is buried among the hazel trees and the mimosas. And wherever he goes, he will throw open the windows onto a garden or, as in Deauville, onto that thing which is implicit and yet hidden in every garden: the ocean.

All gardens long to be reunited with the sea. Slip the leash and, in an instant, they will hurdle the fence, the high walls of time, moving quickly despite pockets stuffed with stolen plums and apples, for behind its mask of studied civility, a garden is a mischievous child. This is true of all gardens, every single one, if they are left to their own devices, if we do not stare at them with the fixed grin of a lawnmower, the scowl of a pair of secateurs, the raised eyebrow of the architect planted in the undergrowth like a compass rose on a map.

Ask Pierre, who took his first steps in a garden, gazing over the green waves suffused with light; Pierre will tell you that all gardens tend towards the sea. He spent the first eight years of his life – the longest years in the life of any man – in the garden at Fontenay-aux-Roses. In these early years we do not notice the passing time, for this is time that does not pass, it is harvested, gathered in, wheat and chaff together; it is time stored away, the invisible gold of days.

Because the child cannot see that he is a child, or sees it only dimly, faintly aware of it from words he has overheard, the blindness of the adult kingdom repels him. Because a child is the bird that he is watching, and with the bird can fly over lakes and mountains, he prowls with a cat over the rooftops and the gutters, and quivers with the treetops resting against the sleeping forest.

Pierre was only eight years old when, using the paintbox his grandmother gave him, he first traced on paper the path that leads from the garden to the sea. This was how Pierre discovered America before Columbus.

It is an experience from which you never recover.

A Bonnard Nude

Darkness still unknown,
I want you almost naked
On a black divan.
        Paul Verlaine

2 1

Colour is a woman slow to be seduced, a fleeting glance, a soft caress. From the first it is clear that this will be a ceaseless, endless battle with the light. There will be times when the artist must pretend to surrender, to retreat, to withdraw into shadows, silence, solitude.

For to paint is to give colour voice, to take a perfectly written score and make light sing for the silent, listening eye. So that living flesh can feel at last the joy of living, so that we tremble to hear it laugh as though, thrown into its arms, we wreathed in an instant with our own matchless foliage, with every colour.

22

There is a photograph by Brassaï of Matisse in his studio in 1939. He sits, tie neatly knotted, waistcoat buttoned under a large white open smock. Were it not for the long-suffering nude, standing with her weight on one leg and the half-finished canvas on the easel in one corner, the paintbrush, the palette and the untidy sofa, one might mistake him for a country doctor at his surgery taking notes.

The painter's eyes as they look at a model are extra-ordinarily precise. A scalpel point at the meeting of pubis and thighs. For a long time, as he focuses on the luxuriant tuft of hair, Matisse daydreams, but all the while his hand sketches, as though his eyes were in the tips of his fingers.

No one could have taken such a photo of Bonnard. Because he painted standing up, alone, in secret, shut up in his studio, working from rough drafts and sketches. He is a hunter, savage and silent, he sits down only when he wants to contemplate the trophies hanging on the wall or tossed onto the floor: canvases, drawings, sketches, some pinned side by side, others

strewn across the floor, lying open or rolled up. He stares at
them in silence for a long moment, listens as the sketches
talk to one another, some make good neighbours, some bad,
he sits and listens to the light as it argues, and watches as
night begins to draw in.

A hunter is born, not made. It is a talent innate to the
eye, or ear, perhaps even the season. Pierre was born in the
depths of autumn, on 3 October 1867, at Fontenay-aux-Roses.

Fontenay-aux-Roses, a small town on the outskirts of
Paris where burrstone houses wreathed with vines and
wisteria nestle demurely in kitchen gardens and flower
gardens, was where Pierre first experienced colour, this was
his mythical forest, his forest of Brocéliande.[4] His bedroom
was an aquarium where the sky swam through the branches
– not the grey Parisian skies which would mark out his early
work, but a hot powdery azure darting through the wild
creepers.

Every childhood, even the most hellish, contains a kernel
of paradise small enough to slip into a trouser pocket like a
handkerchief. Some use it to wipe away their tears, others
to preserve scents and perfumes, or like squirrels to hoard
their meagre treasures: a pebble, a lizard's tail, a slow worm,
a few blades of grass – those things which shape a man's
memory more than all the books, the cathedrals and the
museums of the world.

Every day, at dawn, Pierre the hunter goes into Paris to check his snares, as traders are setting out their stalls, as the milkman is doing his rounds, as the postman, the newspaper seller, the washerwoman and the basket mender go about their business.

Pierre is patient, he knows the paths his prey will take, knows in which café to wait for them to emerge from their lairs. Meticulously, he makes a note of the weather, for weather is the arbiter of colour, it brings colours together and according to its whim can make grey iridescent, cast a patina over pink, set red ablaze.

23 January, *fine*, but already by 24 January, *overcast*. It is enough to adjust ones eyes as one might adjust the sights of a rifle. By being prepared, the hunter increases the element of surprise, should he lose his composure he would lose the very essence of this miracle. He knows that no two skies are alike, knows that each day he must become a different hunter.

When at last his prey appears, surprise intensifies the thrill which inflames the colour. The painter takes aim, he does not need to raise his weapon, his trigger is the blink of an eye and in an instant his quarry is stowed in memory. It does not matter that, by the time he starts to sketch, the woman, the horse, the little girl in pink have flown like a flock of sparrows; it does not matter that the scene has changed, the hunter is no longer watching. But in that instant and for a thousand years, he was a blind man regaining his sight.

Back in his studio, he need only open his sketchpad, blink again, and in an instant the veil is torn, the scene comes to life. He cuts a canvas and tacks it to the wall, with a few dabs of colour the sketch is transferred to the canvas, the horse's nostrils flare and quiver as he snorts at the woman who is staring at the little girl in pink, laughing as she runs.

They are here forever in this museum. And today, one more tomorrow it is I who sits behind the café window staring out at them. The carriage wheel seems ready to roll out of the painting. Time no longer exists. I am blind and I see all that I hear.

23

From the first, Marthe accepts that her role is not to pose for Pierre, but to live by his side. Simply. Tenderly.

Of those rare creatures who pose for him, Bonnard asks only that they say nothing, that they be natural, that they forget themselves and listen only to their instincts. This is not a classroom, there is no teacher here except the light.

Pierre is not content with easy targets, with shooting sitting ducks. He looks for the movement, the artlessness, the spontaneity that is life, just as he did when he was a boy watching goldfish dart through the dark waters of the pond, watching the cat's fur bristle as it arched its back, the horse galloping and the hens pecking on the lawn. He would watch the colours and the leaves in the breeze, the skirts of the servants at Grand-Lemps, the coil of smoke rising from his father's pipe, everything slipping gently into the night.

24

Before Marthe, Pierre's paintbrush had never undressed a
woman.

There were women, many women – wearing gowns or
bathrobes, or bodices, wearing hats, bareheaded, coy or – on
occasion – brazen, like the laughing girl, blonde, flirtatious,
sparkling in the poster for *France-Champagne*. But never before
had there been the suggestion of an ankle, a leg, a breast.
Never a nude.

For a long time, Pierre painted only friends and rela-
tives during his holidays at Grand-Lemps: his grandmother,
his mother, his sister and his cousins, and the servants.
Being short-sighted, colours came to him before shapes,
and so he painted them from a distance, tiny figures against
a mass of trees or meadows, against the façade of the house,
sitting at a table or in the red shadows thrown by the lamplight.

It is hardly surprising that as a shy adolescent, he was
flustered whenever his female cousins leaned across him,

laughing, to see what he was painting. It was rumoured that he fell so in love with Berthe Schaedlin – the girl who sways her hips with such voluptuous elegance in the four panels of *Femmes au jardin* – that he asked for her hand in marriage. But the Schaedlin family would agree only if Pierre would give up this so-called profession in favour of 'a respectable career'. Pierre, proud and resolute, told them: *nothing could cause a painter to give up painting.* If there were tears then, reproaches, hand-wringing, Pierre did not go back on his decision, and the daisy petals that surrounded Berthe's face withered suddenly.

The painting, however, lives on, as do the flowers in the portrait he painted of Berthe in 1892, tender and intimate as a goodbye kiss: the wild red curls, the freckles, the defiant pink lips, the eyes filled with tears that will flow forever on the far side of the canvas.

Barely a year later, Marthe will catch the bouquet.

As for the female models at the Beaux-Arts and the Académie Julian, they are barely worth mentioning, they are no more than the skin and muscle needed to flesh out a skeleton, they assume a few classical positions, a few limber poses, while he learns to sketch. But even afterwards, Pierre still finds it difficult to sketch a bare foot. Fortunately, in the streets of Paris the women all wear shoes. Three cheers for the errand girls, the dressmaker's apprentices, the laundresses, the costermongers, three cheers for well-heeled ladies in hats and veils and three cheers for the consumptive whores. There will be time for nudes tomorrow, when we are handsome, when we find love.

Here is Marthe, it is tomorrow.

25

Marthe has no need to thread artificial flowers onto wire stems now that Pierre pulls more-than-real flowers from his sleeves to toss into her lap; now that in two brushstrokes he can braid wreaths, and cause tremulous lilacs and poppies to bloom and blush beneath her skin.

For as long as Pierre gazes upon her again and again, drinking in her beauty, making her bloom night after night, Marthe will stand naked before him, a nude prized, surprised, captured.

nude on the bed after lovemaking, voluptuous, indolent, a hand caressing the breast from which her pleasure slowly ebbs . . .

half-naked, slipping on her stockings, fastening the red suspender garter, her leg ripe for sin . . .

nude in black stockings in the lamplight, and more naked still, her head caught in the froth of her blouse, abandoned to her blushes,

nude at her *toilette*, a water-nymph leaning over the mirror of the water . . .

nude, washing herself in the half-bath, crouching, kneeling, bent . . .

nude in the long bath beneath the green water, dreamy . . .

nude, standing at the washbasin, in high-heeled shoes, or bending to wash her leg, to clip her toenails, nude and arched, all the gold of days ablaze upon her skin . . .

nude, rubescent and languorous, rolling the sulphurous dreams of Verlaine's *Parallèlement* on her hips like cigarettes . . .

Chloë nude before Daphnis in the pages of Longus,

pink or blue or green or yellow, so naked that the light cannot credit it, nude before the mirror, at the washbasin, framed against the sunlight,

nude with a washcloth, with a quilt, in a fur hat, with a dog,

nude in pencil, charcoal, gouache, in watercolours and in oils,

nude in bronze

forever nude, at any hour, until the end of days,

nude forever young and graceful as though time had stopped for her, for him, on the day when in his shabby room he saw her step from behind the screen

nude, by happy chance, by Bonnard, nude

Marthe, nude, in one hundred and forty-six paintings, Marthe nude in seven hundred and seventeen sketches, drawn on the air, lost in the trees, caressed by the waters,

Marthe, nude at the age of thirty-two, eyes lowered, eyes closed, keeping her secret,

undressing Marthe.

26

A woman at her bath is a joy that begs to be touched, it is a sunny spell amid the dark flesh of the hours, the end to fear. It is *Finnegans Wake⁵*, the heart beating in the toes, the rush of thoughts and dreams, her sparkling beneath the foam. It is the sky turned inside out like a glove, the white mingled with the pink and blue of glad tidings. It is Apollinaire in his vowels, Max Jacob in love and improvising, and the bubbles burst against her skin. It is the marriage between literature and waters. Everyone is here, every man jack, Ulysses has captured Moby Dick, we are back at square one.

Quiet please, rolling. Marthe, scene 2, take 1.

Black is a Colour

In our shadows, there is not one place for Beauty. Every place is for Beauty.

René Char

27

What is most arousing about stockings is the stocking-tops. This line where white flesh peeks out of black silk can set a young man's heart racing as a hare darting from cover can startle a hunter.

It is 1880, Pierre is thirteen years old. Hemlines are low this year and boots are worn high. He watches as the impish wind whips at the hems of the shop girls hoping to catch a glimpse of calf, a flash of the glory of black stockings beneath their fluttering white petticoats. No more dreaming of patrician women in stockings patterned with fleurs-de-lis, of bourgeois calves in prim and proper pink. Dreams now are more down-to-earth. Wool or cotton for the little seamstresses, sheer silk and rucked satin for the ladies and whether lowborn or high, the most fashionable colour is black.

After the humiliating defeat of Sedan, after the horrors of the Commune, Paris has a taste for wantonness. From Pigalle to Montparnasse, in the streets and in the cabarets, soaring hemlines are all the rage and black is the colour that glisters at night, when all cats are grey. Painters storm the heavens of these hemlines with their brushes, and from his perch on a chaise-longue in a brothel, 'Monsieur Toulouse' urges them on.

For his part, Pierre grows up far from such things. He is a good little boy, until Marthe arrives.

They say that the Eiffel Tower is a woman's leg in a fishnet stocking, the four pillars the straps of her suspender belt. They say a lot of things. But that iron leg, so often sneered at, a gift to the city for the 1889 Exposition Universelle, is the most feminine symbol of Paris since Sainte Geneviève.

In passing, let us pay tribute to the memory of Féréol Dedieu – his name, appropriately, means 'of God' – a little-known lingerie manufacturer on the rue Saint-Sébastien. Concerned for women's comfort, it was Dedieu who invented the suspender belt, a minor revolution which will take years to become popular, for the garter is a jealous queen who guards her kingdom in the music hall and in the bedroom.

And it is all the better for Pierre's palette that he has but one motif: Marthe.

Marthe, the lover, has the body of an angel: small breasts, a narrow waist, an arched back, a rounded derrière and deliciously long legs. She likes to fasten her black stockings, which she languorously slips along her thighs, with a flame-red garter as Pierre stands silently watching. In fluttering sketches, drawings, lithographs, watercolours, washes, Marthe stirs the flames, and Pierre throws his most delicate oils onto the fire, immortalising her languid form dressing and undressing with an impish grace and the indolence of a cat.

Pierre's fascination with black stockings remains constant. Between 1893 when he paints *Étude d'une femme aux bas noirs* until 1910 when he completes *Femme aux bas noirs* he will paint *La jeune fille aux bas noirs* (1893), *Femme mettant ses bas* (1895), *Marthe sur un divan* and *Nu aux bas noirs* (1900), *Les Jarretières rouges, Jeune femme assise sur une chaise longue* (1904), and *Les Bas Noirs* (1909), and he will continue to be obsessed with them until *Bas* in 1927–8. Aside from Toulouse-Lautrec, Bonnard is the only artist of his age to pay tribute to the black stocking, and it is a homage worthy of Fragonard's tribute to the *chemise*.

The black stocking first appears in Bonnard's paintings when Marthe appears, and over the years the black stocking will ascend and descend the staircase of his art, fire his palette until fashions change and black is replaced with imitation flesh tone – a vile reddish-brown – at which moment stockings disappear completely from Bonnard's work.

Imitation is everything he despises. Long live untrammelled flesh, painted in all its sweaty, quivering imperfection.

28

But a pattern has been established, and even in the later nudes, there is some vestige of fetishism: red high-heeled shoes, black ballet pumps. Some say that the explanation lies in the cold tile of the floors, or Pierre's difficulties in painting feet, but they can say what they like. Pierre's eye is that of a voyeur who looks – and does touch.

An eye which delights in the juxtaposition of black and white, of black and pink, of that moment when night stumbles into day, of the vague promise of outlines before they emerge into objects, of the hushed germination of the fruit until at last light falls upon it, rounding and shaping it, the tremulous shadows in the hunter's hide and the sudden appearance of the doe.

Let Galileo go back to his calculations, for children are right to believe that the earth turns because their mother's breasts are round. Marthe, face caught in the blouse she is trying to put on, would blush to see the wide-eyed stare of the child she calls Pierre. He looks as though he is twelve years old, standing before this woman who offers herself completely to the light, he looks as though this is his first time, or his last. In a sense, it is both, and it is this which transforms his charcoal into a velvet spindle embroidering his black with the myriad nuances of flesh.

29

In December 1946, a month before his death, Bonnard – together with Matisse, Braque, Rouault and Atlan – will contribute to an exhibition curated by Aimé Maeght in Paris entitled 'Le noir est un couleur' ('Black is a colour').

Of the nine canvases he will show, not one is predominantly black, not even *Nu sombre*. On the contrary, what dominates in these paintings – *L'Atelier au mimosa, Le Cheval de cirque, L'Amandier en fleur* – are the warm, intoxicating colours of living flesh.

In truth, nothing in his painting is more vital and yet more subtle than his use of black. If the yellow of the mimosa is so yellow, if it billows like a dress, it is because a black wind blusters beneath; if the almond tree is a snowball, it is because black fingers have fashioned it; if the head of the white horse in his stable stares at you so intently, it is because the black of his eyes merges with the deepest black of your darkest nights.

For a painter who loves life as Bonnard does, the only

thing which can support colour, can make it exult, is black, just as a poem can attain its most luminous effect only if it feeds on shadows.

The power of black is strange indeed, and exerts a curious fascination on children, most of whom so fear the dark that they can sleep only with a light on. Although children are life itself, it is neither the yellow crayon nor the red that they pick first at their school desks, but black, to which they are faithful. Though mummy may disagree, though the teacher may boom: *Black is not a colour*, they go on scribbling it over their drawings just the same, with the same joyful obstinacy they show when they splash about in mud.

Like them, Bonnard played with black in his painting. The porcelain dish which served him as a palette was always a muddy puddle into which light, laughing, jumped feet together. One day, while using turpentine to clean it, Pierre will accidentally set fire to his palette and stand in wide-eyed amazement, surprised that the flames did not consume the whole house.

Bonnard understood how to get the best from this colour which complements every other, and reinforces it. He gave to black a sensuality, a depth, a pulse which few of his contemporaries could rival, except perhaps Matisse, who did so by other means, to other ends.

In *La Fenêtre ouverte*, a painting from 1921, a black window-blind cuts off the viewer's gaze like a guillotine, letting it fall roughly into the basket that is the room, where a small black kitten lies sleeping, which Marthe, lying on a folding chair, is stroking. Without this razor-sharp black blade, we should probably have overlooked the essential: Marthe taking a nap, stroking the cat.

30

The sleep that follows lovemaking is long and deep and blessed. But all the while the world turns and passions lurch like a storm-tossed ship on the horizon.

It is a morning like any other and yet it is not the same. Nothing has changed: there are flowers in the vase, daylight at the window, the heart is in its place. What then? The woman sleeping close by is called Marthe.

She has been here, unchanging for so many years, he has painted her, sculpted her, dressed and undressed her for so long that Pierre no longer seems to see her. Something is missing, something he needs if he is to move forward, something he cannot define, but without which he finds himself desolate. It is not the child that they will never have, it is not the light that pours down every day, it is not tenderness nor closeness which they have in abundance. It is like spring arriving unexpectedly and throwing open the shutters one morning without warning, like the stranger who turns your world upside-down, suddenly the heart stumbles, the tears come.

Should he travel, leave everything behind, find a change of scenery?

He did. In 1905, he travelled to visit galleries in Belgium, Holland, Germany, England, Spain, often with Vuillard. He brought back nothing except a small drawing of his friend. Three years later, North Africa, not a single sketch. From Italy and from the United States, he brought back nothing. As though France alone – Paris, la place Clichy, the trees and the skies of Vernonnet, the sea at Varengeville, the banks of the Seine – could touch his heart.

Other bodies then, other smiles, other gestures, other nudes? A number of new models did indeed parade through his new studio on the rue Douai, and later at 21 quai Voltaire. Perhaps he was even briefly infatuated with one of them, Lucienne Dupuy de Frenelle, for example, of whom he painted some twenty portraits including a number of nudes. Perhaps. Pierre is more remote than usual, but every night brings him back as before into Marthe's arms.

Yet not quite as before. He is more sombre, more taciturn, more lost now than ever.

But Marthe is jealous. She wants Pierre all to herself, but he eludes her. She broods, she coughs, she wages war on phantoms. The little savage she once was, the sensual, voluptuous gamine, has, according to some of their guests, given way to a termagant.

FOREVER NUDE

Is it the fact that you are forty, Marthe, that causes you to crumble inside as a house does in a fire, leaving only the façade intact? Or is it that all you can see in Pierre's nudes is the image of another woman, of twenty-year-old Marie, the woman you still hide from him at all costs, the woman that he unknowingly saw, he sensed within you?

It is March 1921 and Pierre is spending a fortnight in Rome. Marthe, whose health is failing, has stayed behind in Saint-Tropez at the home of the Manguins where she and Pierre have been living since December.

Pierre did not mention that he was taking Renée Monchaty with him, a beautiful, bewitching, blonde model he met a year earlier.

Two weeks of freedom from Marthe's stifling presence, two weeks to catch his breath, to breathe the air of streets filled with sunlight and shadows cool as spring water; to be twenty years old again, to stroll along on the arm of a girl in a summer dress, a girl as blonde as Marthe is dark, as joyful as she is cheerless, as luminous as she is gloomy: to lose himself in her eyes never to return, to forget his troubles, his routine. Two weeks in which to fill the gaping void and bring himself back onto an even keel, is both too little and too much for any man. For a man like Pierre, who is both captivated and overwhelmed by the love showered upon him by this passionate woman.

He is loath to go back to Marthe, to take up his lonely life again. And yet already he is crippled with remorse.

Pierre went back to Marthe as though nothing had happened. For to him there is nothing besides painting. Let the day dissolve into a heavy mantle of rain, let passion burn within him, let the whole world crumble. So long as Marthe is here, his work is safe. Marthe is his cornerstone, his linchpin, she takes the darkness upon herself so that Pierre can stoke the fire of his colours. She is the sister soul to his silence, who shields him from visitors and wards off the unexpected; the foremost, the irreplaceable woman, the impossible woman who stirs in him both need and desire for women; she is the invisible that thrills his soul.

Whether shut up in her kitchen or lying in her bath, Marthe is the nakedness from which in his paintings the nude emerges.

Pierre thought about her constantly on the long road home.

32

Pierre, my Pierre. My painter, mine.

It is Renée. Renée who can bear it no longer, waiting for a sign from Pierre, a gesture, the sound of his voice; who wants someone to reassure her that she did not dream this, that something did happen between them in the Eternal City, that she is not wasting away in vain.

Renée who waits, who hopes.

Renée who failed to understand that an artist lives first and foremost for his art, and thrives in solitude as a fish in water. To him she was no more than a bubble on the surface when air was needed, and too much air would make it impossible for him to sink back into the depths where all colours are pure. She did not understand that passion, love, would cause the oceans to spill over and toss him onto the burning shore; that she has come too late, for there is Marthe, and that in his painting, Marthe is the point of no return.

Shortly after Rome, Renée began to telephone him, and Pierre left it to ring, or Marthe answered. One, two, three, ten, how many urgent, breathless, anguished calls tearing her apart? But there is no answer.

Then, there is silence and Pierre feels a sense of mounting dread with every passing day. Al last the terrible news: Renée is dead, she has taken her own life.

Time overflows, wrote Éluard on the death of his wife Nush. Pierre does not write. Shut up in his studio, he staunches his tears in light and paints what is in his heart: Renée and Marthe on the same canvas. The radiance of Renée, smiling, in her lilac satin blouse, wreathed in mimosas and the day's golden sun, setting the canvas ablaze while Marthe, in profile, is a grey Madonna relegated to the corner, contemplating her downfall and weeping for her lost beauty.

The sky has fallen over her like a sheet. Her cough is serious now, and getting worse. Marthe stays shut up in her bedroom all day, as a black wind sweeps through from who knows where, pushing her closer to the edge of this swirling abyss. Now she sees Marie again, the little girl in her clogs, singing through her tears, reminding her how she has lied.

Oh, la menteuse, elle est amoureuse.

Enough. She can bear it no longer, she gets up and in the green water of the tub, in the deep water, drowns her pain and washes her body and her soul.

33

O dreamer, arms resting on the red checked tablecloth, dreamer with your hair of organdie and sainfoin, you who no longer see the things around you. You do not see Black, sitting up to beg for a sugar lump, you do not see the steaming coffee, nor do you roll the hard stone of your pain between your fingers. If you only knew how beautiful you are, how naked in the yellow blouse that reveals your delicate throat, touches your tender lips with a velvet kiss, shows the brazen purple of an erect nipple, if you could only feel the love, beaten and tossed by the winds, that this the man who stands before you feels even now, as he dips his brush into the light of the lamp and of the high windows.

Do you remember the day Thadée surprised Pierre at Vernon? When you heard about it, you smiled, gazing at Pierre, feeling suddenly relaxed and happy. You remember: Thadée ran into Pierre, he was alone in the house, frantic, distraught, his hair wild, his feet bare on the cold tiles, staring into space, oblivious to his guest, murmuring your name over and over *Marthe, Marthe,* only your name, *Marthe,* as though he had lost you, and indeed for a moment, Thadée thought something had happened to you. In fact you were asleep in the room next door, finally asleep after a terrible night through which Pierre sat by your beside, holding your hand.

Do you remember taking the waters at Luxeuil, the cures at Saint-Gervais-les-Bains, at Saint-Honoré, with Pierre by your side, his arm through yours as you walked, smiling, loving and attentive as you negotiated the steep slopes and the brambles?

And do you remember his sensitivity, surprising you one morning when you were low by inviting Louise Hervieu to come especially for you? She too was a painter, and Pierre, who had long known that you longed to learn to paint, thought she would be more capable than he of teaching you. So that you might be a part of him, might know his heart.

Imagine the joy he felt as he listened to the peal of women's laughter from the garden, as he watched you be reborn in light, in your own colours. Imagine.

Life and Death of a Window

The best thing about museums are the windows.
Pierre Bonnard

34

Then the sky opens its eyes once more and spring bounds
through the window with the sea in its arms. Marthe is
dressed again in red and Pierre gazes at her with eyes so fresh
it is as if he gathered them from a nest of Artemisia.

They have just come from visiting Cannet, a villa they
first spotted some time ago, on one of their long walks over
the hills above Cannes. Perched on the hillside, surrounded
by terraced gardens, Cannet looks like the house at Vernonnet
but for the fact that here it is not the Seine but the
Mediterranean which sparkles below, between the umbrella
pines, the acacias and the orange trees, like a lake to which
the mountains of Esterel have come to drink.

In February 1926, Pierre signs the deed before a public
notary to acquire the villa and immediately sets about reno-
vating it according to his own design. On the ground floor is
a vast dining room with French windows opening onto the
garden. On the first floor there are three bedrooms which
face due south: Marthe's is painted in Naples yellow as are

the small salon and the dining room. To the east, painted in blues with wardrobes in white are Pierre's bedroom and the guest bedroom. To the north, Pierre's lofty studio looks out onto the mimosas and to the south-east, the bathroom is tiled in grey-blue. At the foot of the stone steps which lead to the avenue Victoria, a garage has been carved out of the hill for Pierre's new Lorraine-Dietrich, which replaced the Citroën. The exterior is in pink roughcast, there is a south-facing balcony. Electricity, central heating and running water: the renovations take a year to complete.

On 27 February, they move in. Here, too, the furniture is minimal: a few mismatched armchairs, some rattan tables and chairs, one or two old wardrobes, but for the most part it is decorated with the red tablecloths, the Vallauris vases and the baskets of fruit which will appear in Pierre's later paintings and which delight Marthe's eyes and her heart.

It was in 1910 that Pierre first became infatuated with the luminous radiance of the Midi. *What light! Like something from the* Thousand and One Nights. *The sea, the yellow walls, reflections as highly coloured as light itself* . . . Saint-Tropez, Grasse, Antibes, Cannes where they spend their summers, these will eventually lead them to Cannet. Pierre loves the bustle of the port, the fishing boats, the sky over the sea; Marthe prefers the flowers, the fruits, the almond trees and the mistral playing among the palm trees. And more especially, the bracing sea air which revives her and the privacy it affords.

The new house is christened Le Bosquet – The Grove – and they invite a number of their friends – Matisse who lives in nearby Nice, and Monsieur et Madame Hahnloser.

Here, Pierre will paint to his heart's content, here his palette and his sense of wonder will be reborn, here the sunlight of the Midi will prompt him to re-examine everything about his painting, for though seemingly constant it is constantly shifting, hence the daily notes in his diaries detailing the weather. It is his diaries which, when he finally begins to paint – often under artificial light – remind him of the subtle variations each day brings to colour. Hence: *fair weather but chilly, there are traces of vermilion in the orange-tinged shadows and violet in the greys.*

Between 1927 and 1947, more than two hundred and fifty paintings, in oil and in gouache, will be conceived in Cannet: landscapes sunlit and stormy; the garden, painted from every angle, yet always Eden; interiors in which Pierre takes us through every room of Le Bosquet, every room but one: Marthe's bedroom. In these paintings the most mundane objects – the wireless on the mantelpiece, a red cupboard, a radiator – take on a certain grandeur. Still lives one might almost eat, oranges, persimmons, cherries, peaches, grapes, and flowers: peonies, mimosas, lilacs, roses and more roses, and, most vivid of all, Marthe, nude, at her bath, at her *toilette*, Marthe in the dining room, in the small salon, preparing dinner or leafing through a magazine, Marthe with her basset hounds, Marthe daydreaming, Marthe, forever Marthe,

who hides Marie.

35

The year before, on 13 August 1925 to be precise, Pierre married Maria Boursin.

After thirty-two years of living with Marthe, Pierre marries Maria-Marie, because, coming home from a trip one day he finds her in tears.

She was crying because a few days earlier, while talking with her friends, one of them referred to someone she disliked as 'not the kind of woman you'd marry'. Marthe was devastated by the phrase. She thought of all the years she had spent with the man she loved and suddenly she felt old, useless, forsaken and unutterably jealous.

Seeing her in pain, Pierre, to whom the idea had probably never occurred, realised that what Marthe is waiting for could wait no longer. After his affair with Renée, Marthe's insecurities grow like weeds and her depression worsens. Pierre can no longer shirk his obligations. Although she is already his muse, his inspiration, everything that is visible or implicit in his work, clearly Marthe needs a deeper commitment.

The next day, Pierre sets in motion the necessary formalities for making her his wife, and so discovers her secret: Marthe de Méligny does not exist. This aristocratic name, worthy of a courtesan, is not hers; Marthe's true name is Maria Boursin. She was not born in Italy, but in France, in le Berry. Her father was not a count nor an impoverished baron, but a humble farm labourer who probably kept three cows and a few pigs to make ends meet.

Was Pierre brought rudely down to earth, shocked by what he had discovered, or did he smile and nod, knowing that the story was nothing more than a poor girl's attempt to make herself more interesting?

It made no difference. Pierre and Maria were married in secret some days later, in the presence of the Mayor of the XVIII arrondissement, the only witnesses their concierge and her husband. Bonnard's family will learn of their marriage only twenty-three years later, during the heartbreaking trial that will follow Pierre's death.

One window opens, another closes. Marie vanishes behind the bridal veil and Marthe smiles. At last Marie has ceased to exist, she has become Madame Bonnard, she is overjoyed. Though he will always call her Marthe, still a shadow will slip into Pierre's dreams, into his studio, causing his nudes to look up and smile. The shadow of Marie.

36

One window in Bonnard's work is different from every other, different from all those he ever painted. A window which suggests that Marthe's dishonesty wounded him deeply. The window appears in a painting he completed in the year they were married.

At first glance, it seems banal: a closed window, cutting its dark wood frame diagonally across the canvas. On one side, the outside world, the landscape of Cannet, white walls and red tiled roofs scattered between the trees beneath the lowering sky over Esterel. Leaning on the apple-green balcony, a face and two bare forearms: Marthe. On the other side of the window is the room: a table pushed against the window, on the chequered waxed tablecloth are a bottle of black ink, a pen-holder, a blank page, and clearly written, in block capitals on the cover of a thick leather-bound tome, the name MARIE. There is no author's name, but that hardly matters. It is almost certainly Peter Nansen, a Danish writer whose novel, *Marie,* Pierre illustrated using Marthe as his model. It is the story of a girl from the Midi deserted by her wealthy lover who returns to her when she falls ill. Nothing very original.

What is, however, original, is the position of the book as regards Marthe in the painting. The window-jamb divides the painting, setting them in opposition. Outside, to all the world, Marthe. Inside, in the privacy of the room, Marie. Marthe to everyone, Marie to him alone, Marthe exposed, Marie enclosed. No window is entirely innocuous.

37

We do not know what we paint, what we write. We do not know the secret in advance. We trust to the colours, the lines, the words, but what we intend remains hidden. It is only much later that meaning suddenly emerges.

The windows in Bonnard's paintings are a palimpsest. What they reveal is a mask, a screen, and the light in the paintings comes not from outside, but from inside. From the fruit on the table, a white door, a tablecloth, a sheet of paper on which nothing has yet been written. The eye is constantly drawn from the outside world, frozen in its frame like an engraving, back to the room where everything happens.

This is also true of the nudes, which mask nudity itself, veil the quivering flesh beneath the skin and bring time to a standstill. The nudes which Pierre will paint now will never grow old.

Now that they have separate rooms, Pierre draws his wife from memory through the eye of a young man in love. She is twenty, perhaps thirty, nude every day at her *toilette* and fragile, graceful, slender. Remembering her like this constantly reawakens in Pierre memories of the girl from the flower shop on the Boulevard Haussmann, the deceitful girl with innocent eyes: Marie. In Pierre's eyes, time stands still: Venus can put her clothes on, Marthe is stepping out of her bath.

In photos from this period, Marthe appears as a short woman in a fur coat, her face is slightly forbidding, her hair short beneath her hat. It could be a photograph of any middle-class woman doing her shopping. Voyeurs should spare themselves the trouble. He portrays her like this in the 1927 painting *The Red Dress,* hard-faced in a black hat, a white spotted coat, a yellow bag, an umbrella. But the red dress magnifies her and suddenly she is transformed from a nobody into a sombre beauty whom we sense could set hearts ablaze. Pierre's is the eye of a child playing with matches.

38

When he paints her, Marthe is like a closed window, she has no reflection. She never smiles and, in the nudes, we cannot see her face, she looks down or looks away. Sitting at a table, dreaming, her expression is vacant. Standing, she can be seen going about her daily chores, feeding the cat, stroking the dog. She is elsewhere, forever elsewhere, but where? The infinite expression of someone absent, someone who all but melts into the walls.

In *La Femme au chien,* painted in 1940, two years before her death, Marthe is a young girl once more, though here she seems to be in mourning for herself. Hunched over a purple table, she is reading or weeping. Her round face is a mask of heartbroken tenderness. For the first time, silver threads glitter in her hair. Only Poucette, her basset hound, looks at the painter as she hugs him to her breast; his are the saddest eyes in all the world.

It is Poucette who closes the windows.

39

On 26 January 1942, in the dead of winter, Marthe passes away. She is seventy-two. In a coughing fit which rends her body, Marthe finally rejoins Marie.

'My poor Marthe is dead,' writes Pierre to his old friend Henri Matisse, six days after he has buried her in the little cemetery at Cannet.

Pierre's hair turns white with shock. Now he is alone and finally ready to meet the great, gentle, imperious eye of the animal which for so long has been calling to him from deep inside the mirror. It is not a unicorn or some mythical animal, but an ordinary white horse in whose great black eye Pierre can drown his grief.

He first saw the horse in 1934, at the circus in Medrano. Two sketches dating from then appear in his sketchbooks. Two years later, at Deauville, his back to the sea, Pierre begins to paint him in oils: the mountain of snow in the foreground is his head while in the background, as though in hell, other white horses toss restlessly. Frozen like a Christmas ornament in the corner of the painting, the trainer limps, brandishing a whip which looks exactly like a paintbrush, while the horse, indifferent to what is going on around him, consents to lift his hooves one by one. But his eyes are elsewhere, at once fiery, sorrowful and serene. As though he has already jumped every hurdle the world has to offer, has left behind the outward show of the flesh, as though he were a horse only to those with eyes who cannot see.

Pierre's affection for horses is age-old. How many times, when the streets of Paris thronged with carriages, did he stop to stroke their manes, to capture in the horses' green eyes the secret tender gold, whispering words of consolation, he who was always so sparing with his words?

All these things crystallised in the circus horse. Because of the garish lights, the drum rolls, the clash of cymbals, the circus ring where grass has been replaced with sawdust; because of the audience which applauds though they do not understand, because their raucous laughter is a denial of suffering and death, because they have mistaken spectacle for life.

For ten years – between 1936 and 1946 – the circus horse will remain unfinished, pinned to the wall or rolled up in a corner. This hiatus in his output is filled with dark clouds and savage storms. On every side, the folly of mankind awakens: the civil war in Spain, Nazi Germany swooping on a France only just back from its summer holidays, from the beach.

The German occupation disturbs Pierre, hangs over him like a grey-green sky throttling the earth. Deprived of almost everything, he seeks refuge in his art, and leaves his house only for his daily walk and for rare, brief visits. To Nice, in particular, to see his loyal friend Matisse, with whom he carries on a regular correspondence.

On 4 March 1941, Pierre writes to him about the death of Charles, his brother, killed in Algeria: *A whole part of my life has disappeared with him*. Some days later, Matisse informs him of the death of Josse Bernheim, art dealer and a mutual friend. As though sickened by the times in which they live, one after another, they all pass on: Denis, Ker Roussel, Maillol.

In June 1940, the red flame that is Vuillard gutters out, and with his death, Pierre's first studio disappears. Five years later, Pierre will glorify his old friend in the vast *Saint François de Sales bénissant les malades*, painted to hang in a church in Haute-Savoie.

When it comes Marthe's turn to pass away, 'life is broken,' and with it all the windows.

The Butterfly of the Year 2000

The only true paradises are lost paradises.
Marcel Proust

40

Though his tears dry in time, love knows no end, and that which was still lingers in the locked adjoining bedroom. Pierre keeps the key in his jacket, rubs it like a talisman every day before he resumes his work.

Resume, the word says it all, for nothing is ever finished. Those things that make us human are never completed here on earth. Even in death, life goes on. The physical – which is, after all, no more than a well-oiled theatrical device – grinds to a halt, and the body which once we could see, could touch, wastes away, disappears. Like the children of Saint Thomas,[6] we say it is no more.

Few people know how to see, Bonnard would say, *to see well, to see completely. If they only knew how to look, they would better understand painting.*

If they only knew how to see, they would know how to live. How to go beyond the body trapped in the mire. Go beyond the present which encircles and assails them, yet which is no more than Maya,[7] no more than Illusion. They could go beyond the subject of the painting, the forms, the colours, and finally enter into the painting, truly encounter the painter, and by their own means extend his vision. If they but knew how to see, they would not talk of happiness or God; they would use precise terms. They would realise that everything *is* beyond the visible and that nothing which lives truly dies. That behind the sea is the sea, infinite and eternal. Like love.

But we are poor and insignificant. Within us, peering through the black holes of our pupils is an *I* we do not know that sees and sings, but we do not listen. So poets go on crying in the wilderness, painters go on conversing with the deaf who understand them better than those who speak their language, and people prefer the precision of naming to the uniqueness of seeing, they prefer to question rather than to listen with the senses and to accept with the heart, which is steadfast and silent.

In his studio, Pierre spends endless hours gazing at the wall on which nudes talk to landscapes, portraits converse with still lives. Endlessly looking, endlessly listening to the light as it talks to the colours, to that green which yearns to be blue while the complementary red invites a whispered prayer. Then, silently, heart filled with the rustle and murmur of things, he picks up the china plate that serves him as a palette and begins to mix his colours.

41

It is neither colour nor technique that makes a painter, any more than schooling can unmake him. It is the individual way in which they seize the world by the scruff of the neck, holding on regardless of what or who would have them let go. It is the way in which they stop their ears and close their eyes to everything but that still small voice which stirs within them with such force that nothing can prevail against it.

Like children, who since the beginning of time have known that clouds are blue, cows are green and rain is golden, and who, with the impudence of angels, can put the sea into a bottle and set the galleries of the world ablaze, Pierre became Bonnard by listening to his heart, and his hand never betrayed him.

To the end, he never ceased to marvel at the world, to bring time to a standstill, to contend light with light, to re-invent heaven and earth, sea and mountain, man and woman. To sing the love of the world, the joy of living in spite of what he felt, for *to sing is not always to be joyful*.

With a hat upon his head, a scarf about his neck, his jacket buttoned to the throat, he darts round his studio, settling on one painting then another like a butterfly, the tip of his paintbrush leaving behind vestiges of spring that spring has never known. His hands, in stark contrast with his delicate frame, are calloused as a labourer's. Behind his glasses, his eyes are ringed with a fire that can bring whole forests of oak crashing down like a house of cards, or, with a brushstroke, open up glades and dells.

I hope that my painting will survive without cracking, he writes in 1946, *I would like to appear before the young artist of the year 2000 on the wings of a butterfly.*

42

When he has folded up his wings and placed his paintbrush in its box, the butterfly Pierre is nothing but a withered body waiting for night to come and carry him away. *I shall be happy only when I am laid in earth*, he says.

Now that the windows have guttered out, the nights are more vast than the tedium of the day. With Poucette asleep in his lap, Pierre dedicates his time to rereading his favourite writers. Yesterday, it was La Fontaine, and he could not help but sketch some comical illustrations in the margins of his well-thumbed copy; the day before yesterday it was Verlaine, today it is Proust, starting again from the first page of *In Search of Lost Time*; tomorrow it will be the complete works of Mallarmé including his English primer *'Thèmes anglais'*. So much beauty, and yet nothing to console him.

To think that he must live to face another morning, another evening, see himself reflected in the mirror, watch himself shuffle away with short steps and not end it all like Seneca in the bathroom.

Oh Marthe, where are you now? You who played so often in this room. Where are your fiery eyes, your graceful body, where is the time we spent in one another's hearts, and where am I? And under this white mane of hair, deep in these sunken eyes, who am I but an old nag licking salt from the walls, waiting to be taken to the knacker's yard? Who am I that the least glimpse of you can make my eyes grow wide again with joy?

Live — as though one might never die — as though our last day had come.

43

After 1942, Pierre paints many self-portraits using a mirror. They would seem simple, even harsh, were it not for the halo of light which flocculates about them, bathing them in quiet melancholy. As in Rembrandt's self-portraits, only the eyes are questioning, and here they are the eyes of the circus horse.

Bonnard knows that his hours are numbered. He has gone as far as his vision can take him and returned serene. There are colours even in the deepest shadows of *L'Amandier en fleur*, his last painting. It is a heartfelt plea to life itself. The tree in the painting is the end which has no ending, standing as a man might stand. Not any tree, not any man, but a tree that flowers in winter when all about it play dead, a man who puts his greatest light into his shadows, a tree whose clusters of white flowers remind man that life appears only to die. This is the tree which Pierre discovered in the depths of his being, instinctively, unconsciously. He probably did not know that this painting too, like his painting of the circus horse, was a self-portrait. He did not see that the black and gnarled branches of the tree were like his arms, did not see the echo of his white hair in the almond-blossom. No, he simply felt the tree grow within him, its shoots budding through his fingertips, life, which has no end, blossoming.

It's not a matter of painting life, it's a matter of giving life to painting.

On his deathbed, Pierre sent for his nephew, Charles Terrasse, and pointing to *L'Amandier* on the floor he said: *That green, the earth, is wrong, it needs more yellow.* Charles handed him a paintbrush and supported the old man's hand as Pierre, with a single brushstroke, poured onto the ground at the foot of the tree all his life's gold: the field of corn where he and Marthe rolled together, the blaze in the eye of the circus horse, and the wings of the butterfly of the year 2000.

44

The death of Pierre Bonnard at the age of eighty on 23 January 1947 caused little stir in the world of art. It was hardly surprising: he cared little for society, had few friends in the art world, lived like a hermit and was thought a throwback to Impressionism. Aside from articles and obituaries by loyal friends, writers whose lives he had touched, and irreproachable painters like Braque ('Bonnard was pure and true, he was not an artist who played at purity') or Dufy, who speaks of the 'profoundly human genius of Bonnard', there was nothing, or very little, but there were *ad hominem* attacks too, such as the headline in *Cahiers d'Art*: 'Is Pierre Bonnard a great painter?', to which Zervos[8] replied with a peremptory 'No', which immediately prompted Henri Matisse to write in the margin of his copy: 'Yes. I certify that Pierre Bonnard is a great painter of our time and undoubtedly of the future. Henri Matisse, January 1948.'

Although Bonnard had exhibited widely in France and elsewhere since the turn of the century when he met the

Bernheim brothers, art dealers and gallery owners who were to represent him throughout his career; although many monographs about his work had appeared since the first was published in 1919; and although he had been able to earn his living from his art from the age of thirty, still, it would be some time before his own country truly recognised his talent. Even today, his work is poorly represented in French museums compared to foreign galleries where his work was well-received from the first.

Bonnard himself did nothing to improve matters. Quite the contrary: his mercurial and eccentric personality prized freedom above all else, his eye was attracted to the strangeness on the Paris streets, his ear attuned to the plainchant of lilacs and shrubs. He was indifferent to schools, to theories and to fashion, none of which helped his cause in a world where to perform, to dazzle, is everything. Nor was his cause helped by Marthe's jealousy, her possessiveness and her delicate health, though it doubtless shielded him from the squabbles, the scheming and the spectacle of the art world. As interest grew in his work, Bonnard became even more elusive: *I know there is something in what I do, but this is madness . . .*

Constantly wayfaring, he kept a low profile and when, in 1939, he retreated to the Midi, he cut his ties with Paris. But to the end, he would steal back at times, like a thief.

The woman he loved, the colours of the daylight, cats lounging among books, a few friends and the splendour of the world about him, what more could he ask for, what else?

Of course, such art is too innocent, such happiness too naïve, it is an Arcadian dream intolerable to those in Paris breaking their backs to be original, keeping their several irons in the fire of the *salons*, the *revues d'art*, the galleries, painting with any brush that comes to hand in pursuit of absurd glory.

Bonnard's glory, his *raison d'être*, is to paint what he pleases, as he pleases, when he pleases. If that irritates the arbiters of fashion, too bad. In his mouth, pleasure will always have the taste of forbidden fruit: *Draw your pleasure. Paint your pleasure. Express your pleasure strongly.*

In short, Bonnard's only mistake was to become who he was born to be, to be only, to be utterly, himself; to say aloud what most no longer dared to think: that happiness, that love, that beauty exist, which is neither *avant-garde* nor *arrière-*. To say that it is a joy to spend one's life seeking out such things. Within oneself. Deep within.

There is no better way to make enemies.

45

The most brilliant of Bonnard's enemies was unquestionably Picasso who was unable to tolerate anything which challenged him, anything which he could not twist or subvert and integrate into his own work, anything that did not stimulate him and give his work new impetus.

His comments on Bonnard — among others, for few of his contemporaries were spared his critical spleen — were brutal. And yet whom should a gallery owner surprise one morning poring over paintings in a Bonnard exhibition but Picasso, who had publicly excoriated the same exhibition only the night before.

For his part, Bonnard never ceased to be fascinated by the work of his contemporaries. In quiet moments he visited museums and art galleries, felt humbled by the work of some and laughed at the pretentious bombast of others. *It's nice to get up on your hobby-horse*, he noted, *but it's best not to think of it as Pegasus*. And he never forgot the practical advice given him one day by a house painter: *Monsieur, in painting, the first coat is always easy, I'll wait and see the second.*

In his studio, above the chest of drawers littered with bottles of turpentine, jars filled with brushes, rags, the wall is papered with maps, reproductions of paintings, silver wrapping paper on which reflections of daylight dazzle one another. Here and there, between a postcard-sized Vermeer and a Cézanne, towering over them all by virtue of its size, is a Picasso. *This man's eyes are not like other men's,* [9] he said one day to the amazement of his grand-nephew Michel Terrasse.

A tribute from the French butterfly to the Spanish bull.

We are never so eloquent about ourselves as when we talk about others.

The Pleasures of Lying

The incredible is often truth itself.
Pierre Bonnard

46

There is an expression which applies perfectly to painting, wrote Bonnard: *many little lies can make a great truth.*

What is true of painting does not necessarily apply to society. Seven months after his death, Pierre Bonnard was in trouble with the law, posthumously accused of making false entry and of possession of stolen goods – his own paintings.

It is the height of absurdity. The law is quick to blunder and the greater the blunder the less likely it is to realise it.

In fact, since his marriage to Maria was *sans mariage contrat*,[10] all assets were necessarily jointly owned with Marthe, so he was legally obliged to declare his wife's heirs. Distraught after the death of Marthe, Pierre, who knew nothing of such red tape, did nothing. Later, on the advice of his lawyer, and to avoid any administrative problems, he quickly wrote a false will which he signed on behalf of Marthe, but grief-stricken and inattentive, he made the mistake of appending the date on which he wrote it: 11 November 1942 – almost nine months after her burial.

What his lawyer failed to spot did not go unnoticed by the legal system.

47

It all came down as it always does to money. It must be said that what was at stake was considerable: six hundred paintings, five hundred watercolours and more than five thousand unpublished drawings by Bonnard.

Having tried in vain to set Bonnard's heirs against one another, the art dealer assigned to the case joined forces with the family lawyer to seek out the heirs of Maria Boursin. In doing so, he discovered the fake will and pressed charges which led to the trial in which Bonnard was post-humously convicted for making false entry and recieves stolen goods.

There was worse to come. It was now that Marthe's deceit reached its apogee: the fictitious aristocrat had heirs, though she did not know them any more than they knew her. Tempted by the prospect of such a fabulous legacy – though they did not give a fig for art, and had never even heard of Bonnard – these heirs suddenly proved to be extraordinarily greedy. The heirs were Marthe's four nieces who lived in

Marseille. Not content with claiming their part of the estate, they asserted rights over all Bonnard's work.

The proceedings would go on for twenty years.

The villa at Cannet, placed in sequestration and left to the tender mercies of time and thieves, went to rack and ruin until Bonnard's nephew finally managed to buy it in 1968; restored the villa to its former glory and succeeded in having it made a listed building in 1974.

As for the paintings, they were locked away in four bank vaults, for two decades they would not see the light of day so dear to Bonnard.

Little lies sometimes go to make a great truth. Thus it was that the 'affaire Bonnard', as it was known, resulted in a law being passed which finally guaranteed the artist sole and entire rights in his work.

48

The man who always thought there were 'too many zeroes' on the cheques art dealers were so keen to give him, who even insisted on subtracting some of them; who decided *out of a sense of decency* that he would no longer sell his work on the day he discovered the breathtaking sums his paintings were fetching, such a man would have found this rank display of greed, folly and malice over his work intolerable.

For Bonnard, there was a limit beyond which trade was undignified, grotesque, a limit beyond which art became simply one more product.

The hermit with the butterfly wings could not imagine that something as vibrant, as alive as a painting could languish in a bank vault, snatched from the daylight, from the eyes of living, since deprived of light, all things wither, all flowers, all women, all joys,

and the idle thoughts that roam the streets,
and the songs, lulled by the breeze, grow bitter and biting
as knives.

Paintings, too, grow bored in galleries, when visitors stay
away and sunlight wanes. Curators know this and these days,
the moment that a painting begins to wilt, they quickly send
it out to take the air, despatch it across the seas, to be seen
by other eyes in distant lands.

49

One last image: a little man in a raincoat and a hat wandering through the musée du Luxembourg with his friend Vuillard. The year hardly matters, but the sunlight streaming through the windows is clement for the season. Suddenly, he stops in front of a painting, his brow furrows. He steps back, looks at the painting from a different angle, but still he is stunned by what he sees.

Distract the guard, he says to Vuillard, who reluctantly does as he is asked. From his pocket, the little man takes out a paintbox the size of a pack of cigarettes and a paintbrush barely two inches long. In a flash he has retouched the painting, pocketed his materials and no one is any the wiser. He smiles. Rejoining Vuillard, who is still talking to the guard, he takes his friend by the arm and leading him away explains: one of the paintings was dying for lack of yellow, it couldn't hang on much longer. But everything's fine now, let's go look at the springtime.

Vuillard is flabbergasted, he looks at the little man by his side: Pierre Bonnard is ten years old.

Epilogue

There are thousands upon thousands of them wandering the streets, catching the sunshine and the city lights, and in an instant, we who are about to die forget who we are and what we are searching for.

Sometimes, one of us gets up and leaves, as though he had lost his eyes, and disappears into the darkness. I was that man, Pierre, when Marthe first appeared to me.

Between the beauty you unwittingly thrust upon me, and the beauty that you loved for forty-nine years, there is a whole world which has nothing to do with painting.

A whole world which is the adventure of seeing, its shadows and its light, its heartbreaks and its joys. A world that seems to be infinite, and yet like the life of a man, is finite. The keys to this world cannot be found in a book nor in nature, but deep within us, in that place behind our eyes where the garden of childhood waits still, heart racing, yearning for the sea.

This is where we must go.

This is where Marthe found me in the gallery, where she saved me from the solitude and boredom which were slowly killing me.

And when I thought that I, in turn, was saving this unknown girl in a red coat in the street, arrogating to myself your role, it was in Marthe's arms that I lay dreaming.

For it is in the nature of dreams for men to save women from some nameless peril. Perhaps it is the beast within. Perhaps it is the nothingness that looms over him, the time which weighs upon him like future generations. Perhaps, he imagines he is saving her from herself, from the lie we call beauty, from her shackles. So that, when he draws her into an embrace, she can deliver this man from sadness and from death and offer him the sea and with it the life-giving salt that is love.

Notes

1 Aurélien Lugné-Poe (1869–1940), an old friend of
   Vuillard, was an actor and director; he founded an avant-
   garde theatrical company, Théâtre de l'Oeuvre, and staged
   the plays of Maurice Maeterlinck, Paul Claudel and other
   Symbolist writers.

   Jean-Hippolyte Flandrin (1809–64), Fernand Cormon
   (1845–1924), Jules Bastien-Lepage (1848–84), Carolus-
   Duran (Charles Durand; 1837–1917) and Léon Bonnat
   (1833–1922) were established painters, who all came to
   devote themselves largely to portraiture, and were despised
   by les Nabis who saw them as ultra-conservative.

   Louis-Adolphe Thiers (1797–1877) was a French
   politician alleged to have ordered the massacre of 'la
   Semaine sanglante' (Bloody Week) during the Paris
   Commune. Thousands of Parisians were killed in the
   fighting, or court-martialled and executed. It is in fact
   more likely that the atrocity was carried out by the army
   and he merely stood back and did not involve himself.

Jean-Louis-Ernest Meissonier (1815–91) was a highly successful Classicist painter and sculptor; William-Adolphe Bouguereau (1825–1905), also a very successful painter, fell into obscurity as the Impressionists gained public recognition.

2   In the Bible Susanna was the virtuous wife of a wealthy man called Joachim. One day, as she was taking a bath in her garden a pair of passing elders spotted her and propositioned her; when she refused they threatened to declare that they had seen her with a young man, a lover, under a tree. Still she resisted and she cried out for help, but the elders were judges by profession and she was beautiful – when the case was heard she was sentenced to death. At that point Daniel interrupted the proceedings and insisted that the two elders should be questioned separately – when their accounts of Susanna's supposed dalliance failed to agree, Susanna was declared innocent and the elders were stoned.

3   A reference to Bonnard's *Femmes au jardin*.

4   Brocéliande – an ancient forest in Brittany believed in medieval times to be a place of magic and mystery. In Arthurian legend it is the setting of several of the knights' quests, and is supposed to be the last resting place of Merlin.

5   The character of Kevin in *Finnegans Wake* retreats to his

bath where he can isolate himself from the rest of the world.

6 The 'children of St Thomas' – the Christians of St Thomas or St Thomas Christians, the Christians of the Indian subcontinent where the apostle St Thomas spread the gospel circa AD 42–9.

7 Maya – put simply, in Hinduism, the deity governing illusion – and illusion is something to be seen through.

8 Christian Zervos (1889–1970), A French art collector, critic and author who founded the magazine *Cahiers d'art*.

9 'Cet homme-là n'a pas les yeux faits comme tout le monde': a reference to the Curé d'Ars (St Jean-Baptiste-Marie Vianney, 1786–1859) : 'Le Curé d'Ars n'a pas les yeux faits commes les autres.'

10 'Mariage sans contrat' – Pierre and Marthe were married without a marriage contract and as Marthe had not written a will, a part of what was considered to be their joint property – which included many unsold paintings of considerable value – could go to her heirs.